Little White Rabbit

KEVIN HENKES

Little
White
Rabbit

GREENWILLOW BOOKS
An Imprint of HarperCollinsPublishers

For Greenwillow—then and now

Little white rabbit hopped along.

When he hopped through the high grass,
he wondered what it would be like to be green.

When he hopped by the fir trees,
he wondered what it would be like to be tall.

When he hopped over the rock,
he wondered what it would be like
not to be able to move.

When he hopped under the butterflies,
he wondered what it would be like
to flutter through the air.

When he hopped past the cat,
he was too frightened to wonder anything—

so he turned around

and hopped and hopped, as fast as he could.

Soon little white rabbit was home.

He still wondered about many things,

but he didn't wonder who loved him.

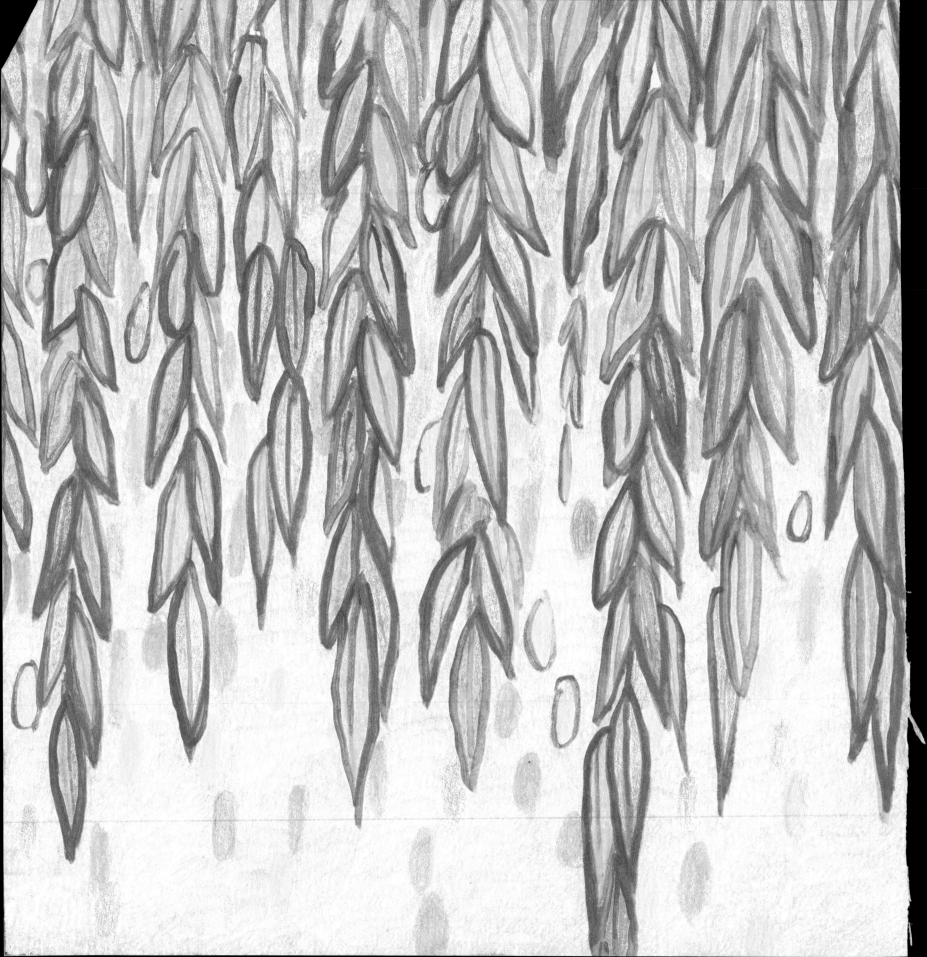